little
Miss
Shy

by Roger Hargreaves

Little Miss Shy just couldn't help it.

Being shy that is.

She was terribly, desperately shy.

She was so shy it hurt.

Which is what they call painfully shy.

If any time at all anyone at all said anything at all to her, she blushed like a beetroot.

She lived all alone in a little house quite a long way from where you live.

In fact, quite a long way from where anybody lives.

Thimble Cottage!

Little Miss Shy was so shy she just couldn't bring herself to leave her little cottage.

She never went shopping!

The thought of walking into a shop and asking for something was absolutely terrifying.

So, she grew her own food in the garden of Thimble Cottage, and lived a very quiet life.

Very, very, very, very quiet indeed.

BANG! BANG! BANG!

Little Miss Shy, who was having breakfast in the kitchen of Thimble Cottage, dived under the table in terror.

But it was only the postman knocking at the door.

"Anybody home?" he called.

Little Miss Shy, under the table, put her hands over her ears and shut her eyes.

"She must be out," thought the postman to himself, and pushed the letter he was carrying under the door, and walked away.

Little Miss Shy waited, and waited, and waited until the sound of his footsteps had died away.

And then she waited some more.

In fact she spent most of that day under her kitchen table!

It was dark by the time little Miss Shy dared to come out.

There it was on the doormat. The very first letter she'd had in the whole of her life.

She opened it, cautiously.

It was from Mr Funny.

'YOU ARE INVITED'

said the letter,

'TO A PARTY'

it went on,

'ON SATURDAY'

it said,

'AT 3 O'CLOCK'.

It added,

'IT'S GOING TO BE FUN! FUN! FUN!'

Little Miss Shy was horrified!

She looked at the letter again.

"I can't go!" she thought.

"I CAN'T!"

"There'll be PEOPLE there!"

PEOPLE!

In the whole wide world there was absolutely nothing that frightened little Miss Shy as much as the thought of PEOPLE.

She worried about it all night long.

But the following morning, she made a decision.

"I'll have to go," she thought.

"It wouldn't be polite not to!"

But, five minutes later she changed her mind.

And, five minutes later she changed her mind back again.

But, five minutes later, guess what happened?

That's right!

She didn't sleep that night at all.

The following day was Friday, and that Friday little Miss Shy changed her mind one hundred and forty four times.

That's how many five minutes there are in a day!

She was going to the party!

She wasn't going to the party!

She was going to the party!

She wasn't!

She was!

She wasn't!

She was!

It was a long day!

And that Friday night was even worse than Thursday night had been. She didn't sleep a wink. Not even half a wink.

Saturday morning came.

And went.

Saturday lunchtime came.

And went.

Little Miss Shy just couldn't eat a thing.

One o'clock in the afternoon came, and went.

Two o'clock in the afternoon came, and went.

And then three o'clock, the party time, came.

And went!

But poor little Miss Shy didn't!

She couldn't!

She just sat there.

A tear rolled down her cheek.

"Oh I do so wish I wasn't so shy," she sobbed.

Four o'clock came.

There was a loud knock at the door.

Little Miss Shy hid behind her chair.

The door opened.

And in walked Mr Funny.

"I knew you wouldn't come," he laughed, looking at her behind the chair.

"So," he went on, "I've come to take you!"

Little Miss Shy blushed and blushed and blushed.

"Come on," cried Mr Funny, seizing her by the hand. "You'll enjoy it once you're there!"

And he marched the blushing little lady off to his party.

Everybody was there!

Little Miss Shy didn't feel very well.

But, everybody talked to her, and everybody was very nice, and gradually, the longer the party lasted, bit by bit, little by little, eventually, guess what happened?

She stopped blushing.

And actually started to enjoy herself.

"Told you so," laughed Mr Funny.

Little Miss Shy nodded, and giggled.

She was having the time of her life!

And only blushing a bit.

And do you know who she met at the party?

Mr Quiet!

"I used to be shy like you," he said.

Little Miss Shy looked at him.

"I don't believe you," she giggled, and then she thought.

"Would you like to come to Thimble Cottage for tea tomorrow?" she said.

Mr Quiet looked at her.

"Me?" he said, blushing like a beetroot.

"Tea?" he said, blushing like two beetroots.

"Tomorrow?" he said, blushing like a whole sackful of beetroots.

And then he fainted!

Fantastic offers for Little Miss fans!

Collect all your Mr. Men or Little Miss books in these superb durable collectors' cases!

Only £5.99 inc. postage and packing, these wipe-clean, hard-wearing cases will give all your Mr. Men or Little Miss books a beautiful new home!

Keep track of your collection with this giant-sized double-sided Mr. Men and Little Miss Collectors' poster.

Collect 6 tokens and we will send you a brilliant giant-sized double-sided collectors' poster! Simply tape a £1 coin to cover postage and packaging in the space provided and fill out the form overleaf.

STICK £1 COIN HERE
(for poster only)

Only need a few Little Miss or Mr. Men to complete your set? You can order any of the titles on the back of the books from our Mr. Men order line on 0870 787 1724. Orders should be delivered between 5 and 7 working days.

--- **TO BE COMPLETED BY AN ADULT** ---

To apply for any of these great offers, ask an adult to complete the details below and send this whole page with the appropriate payment and tokens, to: MR. MEN CLASSIC OFFER, PO BOX 715, HORSHAM RH12 5WG

☐ Please send me a giant-sized double-sided collectors' poster.
AND ☐ I enclose 6 tokens and have taped a £1 coin to the other side of this page.

☐ Please send me ⬜ Mr. Men Library case(s) and/or ⬜ Little Miss library case(s) at £5.99 each inc P&P

☐ I enclose a cheque/postal order payable to Egmont UK Limited for £............................

OR ☐ Please debit my MasterCard / Visa / Maestro / Delta account (delete as appropriate) for £....................

Card no. ☐☐☐☐ ☐☐☐☐ ☐☐☐☐ ☐☐☐☐ ☐☐☐☐   Security code ☐☐☐

Issue no. (if available) ☐   Start Date ☐☐/☐☐/☐☐   Expiry Date ☐☐/☐☐/☐☐

Fan's name: ....   Date of birth: ....

Address: ....

....

....   Postcode: ....

Name of parent / guardian: ....

Email for parent / guardian: ....

Signature of parent / guardian: ....

Please allow 28 days for delivery. Offer is only available while stocks last. We reserve the right to change the terms of this offer at any time and we offer a 14 day money back guarantee. This does not affect your statutory rights. Offers apply to UK only.

☐ We may occasionally wish to send you information about other Egmont children's books. If you would rather we didn't, please tick this box.

Ref: LIM 001

Have you discovered the Mr Men books yet?
There are 46 to collect, and when you have
them all this is what you'll see!

Little Miss Giggles says,
"You'll laugh a lot with these little books!"

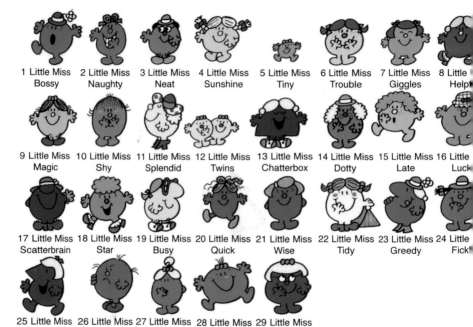

1 Little Miss Bossy
2 Little Miss Naughty
3 Little Miss Neat
4 Little Miss Sunshine
5 Little Miss Tiny
6 Little Miss Trouble
7 Little Miss Giggles
8 Little Miss Help

9 Little Miss Magic
10 Little Miss Shy
11 Little Miss Splendid
12 Little Miss Twins
13 Little Miss Chatterbox
14 Little Miss Dotty
15 Little Miss Late
16 Little Miss Luck

17 Little Miss Scatterbrain
18 Little Miss Star
19 Little Miss Busy
20 Little Miss Quick
21 Little Miss Wise
22 Little Miss Tidy
23 Little Miss Greedy
24 Little Miss Fick

25 Little Miss Brainy
26 Little Miss Stubborn
27 Little Miss Curious
28 Little Miss Fun
29 Little Miss Contrary

30 Little Miss Somersault
31 Little Miss Scary
32 Little Miss Bad
33 Little Miss Whoops

www.mrmen.co

£2.